The Little Bad Book 2

EVEN MORE DANGEROUS!

By MAGNUS MYST

Illustrated by
Thomas Hussung

Translated by Marshall Yarbrough

Delacorte Press

Quick! We have to get out of here! Before they find us!

I mean, hello. Good thing you're finally reading me. I've been waiting for you. I have something super important to tell you!

But we absolutely cannot stay on this page. If we do, they'll find us! I'll explain later. There's no time now. So quick. Turn to page 16 right now and keep reading from there.

Wait—hold on a second. There's one thing you should probably know: my secret is horrifying! If you've already got butterflies in your stomach, you'd better go ahead and put me right back on the shelf. This is no place for scaredy-cats, believe me; what I have to tell you is way too intense. But if you still think you're up for it, then quick:

→ TURN TO PAGE 16 AND KEEP READING!

YOU THINK THIS IS ALL JUST FOR *FUN???*
DON'T MAKE ME

gh!

ha ha ha ha ha

hee hee hee

ha ha ha ha ha ha ha ha

YOU'D BETTER GIVE IT ANOTHER TRY ON PAGE 86.

Whoa. Hey, I knew it. You're all right! Okay then. Let's get down to business:

Do you like boogers? You know that feeling when you dig your finger into your nose and they slide on out? It's fun, **right?** When the thing is finally out of there and you get to fling it off your finger? A great feeling, isn't it?

Just like running around in your old clothes. And getting dirty.

Not at all like combing your hair and getting soap in your eye, right—or do you feel differently?

Thought not.

Honestly, if you don't bathe for three weeks, the worst that happens is you get a few green, fuzzy spots on you. That's all. The smell isn't even particularly bad.

And did you ever hear of anybody who died from burping? Or from smacking their gum? On the contrary. They're actually healthy!

Still, that's all against the rules. Or it's bad behavior. Or "impolite."

Don't you think that's **strange?**

Hey, just what kind of book are you, anyway? What are you trying to tell us? That we should all stop bathing? And eat our boogers? That's disgusting!

Oh no, I totally forgot about her!

That's Sweet Marie. . . .

Somehow I don't seem to be able to do anything about her. She's reading me right now, too. Same as you.

Please! Can you help me get rid of her? I've tried everything!

I really do like being read, you know, but Sweet Marie is a total pain in the neck. She's always complaining about something. And she's always interrupting. Plus she keeps drawing unicorns everywhere. There, you see?

Again!

But I've got an idea! Would you try giving me a really good shake? Maybe it'll make her sick and she'll stop reading me.

Oh you'd like that, wouldn't you! You won't get rid of me that easily. Now come on. Tell a story about ponies. Or something educational. Or I know: something romantic! Oh yeah . . . !

AAAAH. Come on! Shake me! **NOW.** As hard as you can!

FLAA

That's silly. That won't work. I'm still here. Now get back to the story; I don't have much time. I promised my mom I would clean my room. So whatever scary thing The Book of Truth is supposed to have told you, spit it out already.

Oh, you don't have time? What a shaaaame! I'm so, so sorry, but before we can continue, there's still something we have to take care of: a little test! And only someone who's not a dummy will be able to continue. So I'm afraid it could take a while in your case, Sweet Marie. You'd better go clean your room. Like a good little girl.

But thankfully, dear reader, as far as you're concerned, I'm not at all worried: JUST DRAW A LINE CONNECTING ALL THE THINGS THAT ARE AGAINST THE RULES IN ALPHA-BETICAL ORDER. THE ARROW WILL SHOW

YOU WHICH PAGE WE'LL MEET BACK UP ON. I realize, of course, that normally, you're not supposed to scribble in books with a pencil. But trust me. These are special circumstances!

56 · TOOTHBRUSH

· BATH

· FART

SOAP

· BELCH

· SHOWER

99

· EARWAX

SHAMPOO

· TOOTHPASTE

· WASHCLOTH

BOOGER

26

6 · HYGIENE

· COMB

SLIME

24

Oh, so that's what you think, huh?

Really?

Then make yourself

Sweet

comfortable here with

Marie

EITHER THAT OR TURN BACK
AND GIVE IT ANOTHER TRY!
→ ON PAGE 101

15

Good. I knew you were brave. Welcome to my dungeon. They definitely won't be looking for us here. Listen, we can't let them catch us, no matter what. That's why we keep jumping back and forth—to cover our tracks. You understand?

But let's start from the beginning. So:

YOU'RE BEING LIED TO!

And I mean major lies. Whoppers. They're really putting you on! And you probably haven't even noticed yet.

I just found out myself!

I was down in the basement of the library, trying to find some more horror stories, when I came across this giant book. On a pedestal. Wrapped in chains!

Naturally, I struck up a conversation right away. It called itself The Book of Truth—and it claimed it knew all the truths of the universe. So when I asked it to tell me one, you know, kind of as proof . . . it came right out and told me something completely unbelievable! It said that . . . that, um . . .

Wait a second! You've already shown that you're not a scaredy-cat. But how can I really be sure you're not one of them?

Hmmm.

I'd better test you!

What's the best way to do that?

Hm. Hmm. Hmmm.

Okay, I've got an idea! So: Go get yourself a pin. Then stick it in your . . . um . . . in your finger. Yeah, that's right, and then squeeze out a small drop of blood. Let it drip into the circle on the next page.

But make sure you don't spill any, or you'll stain my pages. Hmm, you know what, actually, that's no good. Then nobody could read me properly anymore. Hmmmm.

No, wait!

I've got a better idea! Maybe we'd better do a kind of test that won't get my pages dirty. Here:

LOOK AROUND THE DUNGEON AND CHOOSE THE
THREE THINGS YOU THINK ARE MOST FUN. ADD
THEIR NUMBERS TOGETHER.

If you're not one of them, you're sure to find the
page number where the story continues:

$$? + ? + ? = PAGE NUMBER$$

Phew, that was close! I'm telling you, we really have to be careful!

But I can tell you more in here.

So: you've probably got an idea already of who it is that's after us, don't you?

Who's always forbidding everything? Like burping and nose-picking and gum smacking? And who's always telling you to be polite and behave yourself?

Right.

The **GROWN-UPS!**

Haven't you ever noticed?

I mean, what's the deal with them? Why are they making up rules all the time? And telling you something's wrong every time you're having fun?

20

They don't like any fooling or messing around. Or talking nonsense, just for the heck of it— that they can't stand. We're only ever supposed to dress properly and be "reasonable."

What are you talking about? Grown-ups just want what's best for us!

"What's best for us"—what a crock. Let me tell you both: there's something totally crazy going on.

Just take a look at what they eat! Barley soup! And olives. **YUCK!** Some of them even like broccoli! And endive salad. I mean, would you eat something like that if you had a choice?

And the things they drink! Bitter coffee. Or sauerkraut juice! Have you seen them? They actually drink that stuff!

And then those weird clothes they wear. Button-down shirts. High-heeled shoes. Neck-ties. Who would wear clothes like that voluntarily? They're totally uncomfortable!

And they're always tired and stressed out. Why is it that they spend all their time working instead of doing fun stuff?

I know that one! That's easy: money! They have to go to work to make money.

Oh yeah, Miss Smartypants? Then maybe you can explain this to me: If I made all that money, then I'd immediately buy all the chocolate I could get, right? And a bunch of cool toys. But they spend it all on completely boring things like "insurance," "rent," or "taxes."

Oh, that's ridiculous. They're not doing that because they want to, they're doing it so that we have a comfortable home to live in.

Pshh, sure—so how come they don't build any hidden doors or loop-de-loop slides in these comfortable homes of theirs? Can't they at least let themselves have a little fun at home? Or another thing: Why don't they let kids drive cars? Don't you ever wonder about that?

Is it because kids are too small? Well, why don't they just build smaller cars, then? It can't be that hard, can it? Gas, brakes, steering wheel. When you ride a bicycle, you've got to keep your balance, too—that's even harder!

No, I'm telling you, there's something here that's just not right. But before I can tell you what it is, there's something else you have to do.

You're just trying to string us along!

No, it's got to be this way. For your own safety. And to make sure the grown-ups don't find us. *I've written the next page number in code on the wall.* It's a puzzle that grown-ups regularly fail at. I'm not so sure about Sweet Marie, either, but you, dear reader, are sure to have no problem with it:

Bravo! You must be really smart. Awesome! Hopefully we're clear of Sweet Marie now.

Before you continue reading, though, you should take note of a few things:

 It's important that you **not draw any attention to yourself** while you're reading me. If you get scared, limit yourself to goose bumps. No screaming or sobbing.

 When you set me aside, hide me well. If it's during the day, put me somewhere inconspicuous, like next to a few other books. At night, you'd better keep me under your pillow.

 Don't tell anyone that you're reading me!

At most your best friends, but that's it. More about that later.

 And if you get scared or notice that your head is spinning, like you're starting to go insane, don't blame me. You said you were brave.

Are you finished yet? Tell us about this incredible thing you're supposed to have found out.

Oh no. She's still here!

Of course I am. Did you think you could ditch me with those cheap tricks of yours?

Tell us, already! You're just trying to keep us in suspense so we don't stop reading you, isn't that right?

That's how it was the first time, too. You wanted more than anything to be a big grisly old tome. With lots of dog-eared pages so everybody could see how beloved you were. This is just another one of your attempts to become a big bad book, right? Admit it!

Nonsense.

This time it's serious! This isn't a joke, you'll see! If they ever— Hey, what was that

Did you two hear that?

There was a noise!

What noise? I didn't hear anything.

There was a noise, all right!

Just listen for a second!

They're after us!

QUICK, BACK TO ONE OF MY DUNGEONS.
ON PAGE 20! We'll be safe there for now.

Got your foil hats on? Then listen closely. I'll tell you a story:

One day, not too long ago, a boy named Max borrowed his father's drone. You know what I'm talking about—one of these expensive flying things with a camera, and a screen built into the

remote that lets you see what it's filming. His father hadn't given his permission, of course. But that night, he and Max's mom were both at school for a PTA meeting. So Max and his two best friends, Rico and Daniel, had the whole evening to take the drone out for a spin.

They flew it around the neighborhood and discovered hidden backyards and side alleys. Once some grandpa shook his fist at them. Another time they chased a cat behind some trash cans. Eventually, they even managed to get the drone to do a flip. In short: it was incredibly fun.

Then Max got an idea. They could check out what was going on at the PTA meeting. After all, none of them had ever been to one.

And so, a short time later, they were lurking outside the school. The windows were lit up.

Strangely enough, though, the whole place seemed empty. Once they were sure that no one was around to see them, Max steered the drone up into the night sky.

Humming quietly, it approached the windows. But to their surprise, they saw only empty classrooms. One deserted room after another. Weird. Where was everybody?

"Maybe in the auditorium?" Rico said finally.

There were no windows in the auditorium, but there was a little hatch under the roof that you could see through.

Max worked the joysticks, holding his breath. It was painstaking work, and they all let out a sigh of relief when finally the drone was perched on the roof ledge. They watched the monitor, captivated. And sure enough, there were the adults! They were sitting there in the auditorium and listening to the principal up on the stage. She had a large pointer and was tapping it on a screen showing the image of a student Max recognized: Tessi from fifth grade. The principal seemed pleased; she was smiling. She pointed here and there. Unfortunately, the drone's microphone was too weak to pick up what she was saying. But when she was finished speaking, they could hear clearly that the room had broken out in applause, and on the screen a little heart appeared over the image of Tessi.

"What, that's how they do it?" Max cried in astonishment. Then the next image appeared.

"That's me!" Daniel cried in horror. And sure enough, their mouths hanging open, the three friends saw a picture of Daniel wearing just his underwear. Daniel almost died of shame.

Again the principal pointed and gestured. This time she didn't seem quite so excited. She kept shaking her head. The audience looked skeptical, too.

"What are they doing?!" Daniel exclaimed. He could feel all the eyes looking at him.

Finally, the principal shrugged. A large question mark appeared over Daniel's image. Then she said something else, and everyone laughed.

"What? Why are they all laughing? And what's that question mark supposed to mean?" Daniel was so worked up he was shaking.

Then the next image appeared. A boy from eighth grade. It was immediately clear that things looked bad for him. The principal seemed to get angrier and angrier. And disdainful boos and indignant whispers could be heard from the crowd.

Finally, the principal shook her head and a word appeared on the screen in large type: "FAILURE."

The three friends watched in disbelief as the grown-ups examined one student after the next. So this was how PTA meetings worked? This was horrible!

Then the lights came back on. The teachers were handing something out. From a distance, it looked like pickles. The grown-ups devoured them as quickly as they could, and then . . .

Hold on a second.

There's one thing I have to make clear to you: for real, after this there's no turning back. Seriously. If you keep reading, you'll learn the whole truth. Then nothing will be as it was before, and your whole world will be turned upside down.

So think long and hard. What do you want to do?

I have a nice life. I'd like to remain clue-less.

—> *THEN PUT ME AWAY AND NEVER THINK OF ME AGAIN.*

 Come on, tell me: What did the friends find out? I want to know!

—> *KEEP READING ON PAGE 46.*

Believing is nice.

But you should be **sure!**
After all, we're dealing with an

ALIEN
INV

here.

so go back
and try again
on page 86.

Awesome! You figured out the mirror images!

Very good. But before I tell you the whole truth, you urgently need a foil hat. So, first things first: go get yourself some aluminum foil. To the right, I've laid out steps for how you put the hat together.

I'm not wearing any crazy foil hat!

Ugh, Sweet Marie. There's really no getting rid of you, is there? Fine, leave it, then. If you want to let your brains get fried, go ahead. Whatever you want.

Hmm. Okay. But only because it's for safety reasons. Safety first, my mom always says.

WHEN YOU'RE BOTH FINISHED, PUT YOUR HATS ON AND TURN TO PAGE 30. There I'll tell you what's going on.

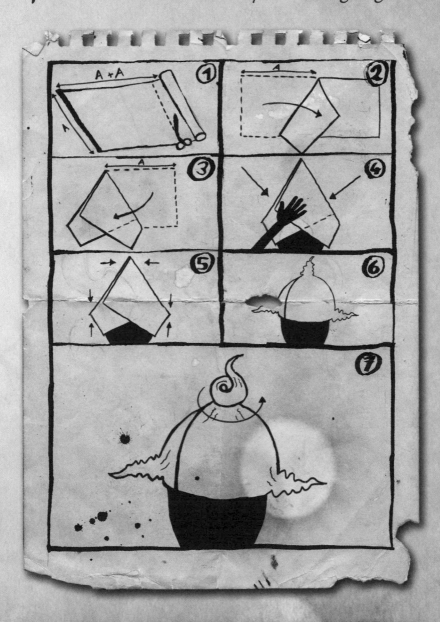

The tubes and pipes wound around the cavern like veins. They all led back to the crystal. They let out sounds—rushing, gurgling, and bubbling—and some of them oozed purple slime. When Phillip got curious and put his hand on one of the pipes, he felt a pulse like the beating of a giant heart. Frightened, he pulled his hand away and took a step back.

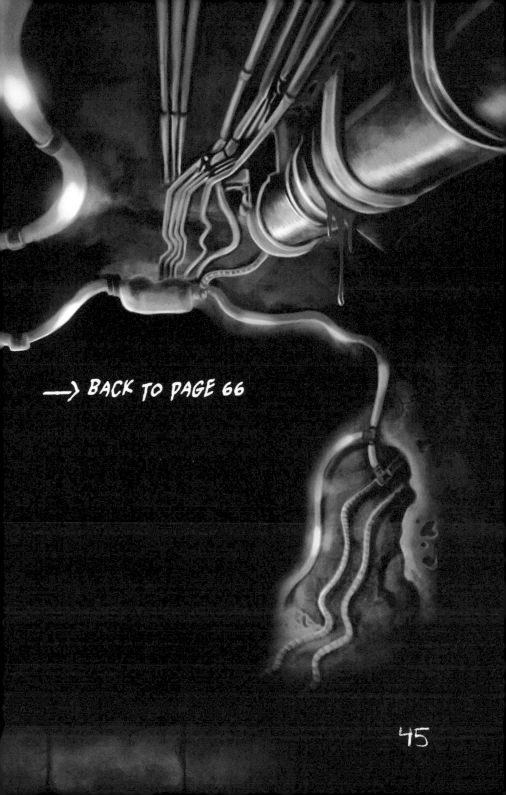

BACK TO PAGE 66

→ BACK TO PAGE 66

All right. If you're sure that's what you want. Read on:

The three friends looked on in amazement as the grown-ups greedily scarfed down the pickles and licked their fingers afterward, as if they'd just eaten some kind of wonderful candy. Then they began to sing.

At first it was just a quiet humming. But it grew louder and louder, and more and more voices joined in. Then it became a howling. It sounded awful, and was completely off key.

What was going on in there? They had never heard anything like it. They couldn't believe their own eyes at first. But soon enough the three friends were staring at the monitor with eyes bulging and mouths agape. For with horror, they saw that the grown-ups' heads were getting bigger and bigger, as if somebody were pumping them up with air! And then they took on the shape of giant BRAINS, with pulsing veins and a green glow coming from within!

Daniel, Max, and Rico felt sick to their stomachs, but they couldn't take their eyes off the screen. Entranced, they watched as the grown-ups' arms and legs began to change.

They started turning soft and green, and repulsive suckers grew on them—all of a sudden, left and right, green TENTACLES came shooting out of the grown-ups' sleeves and pants legs. They twirled them merrily in time with the hideous croaking song, and from their mouths dripped long threads of disgusting purple slime!

STOOOPP! Have you lost your mind?! Just what kind of story is this? This is terrible! You can't tell a story like this!

What do you mean, I can't? Don't you see? I HAVE to! Sorry it doesn't suit you, princess, but no matter how much it hurts, you two are finally going to have to learn the truth:

And the truth is that, in reality, grown-ups are nothing but super-nasty, super-gross

EXTRATERRESTRIALS!

Yes, from space!

And they came here in their spaceships to turn us all into slaves!

You're crazy! "Extraterrestrials." You just made that up!

There's no such thing as extraterrestrials. And school is a nice place. The teachers just want us to learn things so we don't go on being dumb babies forever. And so we can make something of ourselves someday! Like becoming a doctor. Or a police officer. Or maybe a computer whiz! That's a good thing!

Fine, if that's what you want to believe. It's totally up to you.

What do you think, dear reader?

You get to decide: Would you rather live in a world full of pink velvet and glitter, where everything you see is just a lie, put on for show? If so, all you have to do is stay here with Sweet Marie. You two can drink tea together, and she can show you her poetry journal.

Or do you want to learn more? Then prove it!

When I asked *The Book of Truth* where the extraterrestrials actually come from, it showed me a map of constellations. Once you've found these three constellations on the map, you'll know where the extraterrestrials come from.

THE NUMBERS NEXT TO THE CORRECT CONSTELLATIONS WILL TELL YOU WHAT PAGE TO TURN TO NEXT.

? + ? + ? = PAGE NUMBER

Good. You were able to find the page number.

Phew. Man, she really went off the deep end. Seems like the news about her parents really got to her.

I mean, it is rough.

Just so you know, I've got my fingers crossed that they didn't get to your parents, too.

If they did, though, be brave. I've got good news. There's something we can do to fight back against these nasty ALIENS!

Yeah, for real!

There's a way we can protect ourselves from these monsters.

But in order to demonstrate that you're ready for this, you have to do something really horrible first.

You have to prove to me that you're courageous enough to fight the extraterrestrials.

And there's only one way to do it: **YOU HAVE TO DOG-EAR THIS PAGE. FOLD DOWN THE TOP RIGHT CORNER.** Do you think you're up to the challenge?

Yeah, I know, the grown-ups are always saying you should be careful when you handle books. But that's exactly the point! You're proving that you're ready to stop blindly going along with whatever they say!

So get to it. Believe in yourself!

LONG LIVE THE RESISTANCE! GO TO PAGE 82

Awesome! That's the right attitude. Let's get right to it, then.

So.

There's a way to defend ourselves from the aliens. The only thing is, we'll have to resort to a very dangerous weapon: **MAGIC.**

Yeah, I know. The extraterrestrials have probably told you that magic doesn't exist. That it's just a bunch of gimmicks, and magic spells don't work. But that's just like everything else they've told you—nothing but lies!

Curses really do exist. That's why the grownups forbid them.

You'll see for yourself in just a second. Because that's exactly how our plan works: you have to recite a magic spell.

A magic spell?! Come on, are you two crazy?! Magic is dangerous! You're not allowed. Not without a chaperone!

Oh no, you're still here! I thought you lost it and took off. Now, please, will you finally go away and clean your room, Sweet Marie? You haven't understood a single thing I've said. "Chaperone," bah! That's the whole point! No one said fighting the aliens was going to be easy. Sometimes you just have to take a risk!

Yeah, but you don't have to risk everything! If my mom knew what you're trying to get us to do here, she would definitely call the police and make a complaint. And then you would be banned, you'd better believe it!

All right, fine, go and tell on us. By the time you do, we'll have long since said the magic spell, right?

So, quickly now. Let's not pay Sweet Marie any mind. You've got some magical talent, don't you? Let's find out. **THREE OF THE FOLLOWING WORDS ARE MAGICAL. IF YOU ADD THEIR NUMBERS TOGETHER, YOU'LL KNOW WHERE WE MEET UP NEXT.** Hurry!

ABRACADABRA = 60

MIMIMIMIMI = 33

OMNOMNOMNOMNOM = 11

XORXZOROZXXA = 8

AWOPBOBALOOWOP = 7

SIMSALABIM = 2

RAMBAZAMBA = 99

HOCUSPOCUS = 40

BAMALAMABAMALOO = 12

? + ? + ? = PAGE NUMBER

Well done! You can put two and two together. You're just the kind of person we need. After all, you can see for yourself that the situation is pretty grim. We used to think grown-ups were totally normal. But they're really **monsters from another world!** That's why they act so funny. Finally, it all makes sense!

And it gets even worse. You won't believe it! Wait till you hear what happened to a boy named Phillip. It's really horrible. Here:

So. Phillip was an incredibly curious kid who always wanted to know everything. He was always raising his hand and asking questions. He was so curious he even annoyed some of his teachers. But he couldn't help it. He just wanted to know how the world worked.

There was one thing that bothered him, though: There were students who liked to sit in the back of the classroom instead of the front. Who seemed not at all interested in what the teachers had to say. Sometimes, some of them even went so far as to not come to class at all. Phillip didn't understand this. How come they didn't like hearing the teacher explain things? How come they snuck out? There had to be something out there that was even more exciting than class. But what? His curiosity was aroused. And there was only one way to satisfy it: he had to give it a try himself.

The very next morning, there was an announcement. They would have a substitute teacher that day. Phillip could hardly believe his luck.

When the bell rang for the end of recess, he didn't go back to the classroom like he usually did. Instead he headed for the bathroom.

He hid there, full of fear, until the shouting in the hallways had died down. Then he crept out on tiptoe and peered down the corridor. Nothing. It was as if the school was deserted.

He let out a sigh of relief. This was really intense, he had to admit. Every sound echoed down the hallways. Sometimes he could hear voices behind the doors. And his heart was pounding wildly.

Then he walked past the door to the basement. He had always wondered what might be hidden down there, but the basement was strictly off-limits. His hand was on the doorknob. He hesitated. If he was caught, he was sure to be kicked out of school. But he was so curious! Should he risk it?

"Guess you don't have the guts," said a voice.

He spun around, terrified. There stood Trixi. She was one of his classmates who always sat in the back row. He stared at her in disbelief.

"You think you're the only one who didn't feel like doing math?" she said, chewing her gum. "Are you about to go check out the basement?"

He opened his mouth, but no sound came out. She just nodded at him. "Good idea. I've always wondered what's down there myself."

Without another word, Trixi reached out and twisted the doorknob. The door swung open and she headed down the stairs, using her phone as a flashlight.

For a moment, Phillip was terrified. But then his curiosity regained the upper hand, and he followed her.

Hearts pounding, they climbed down the stairs.

"Weird. We've got to be three stories down," Phillip said after they'd been walking for a while. "And it keeps on going." A bad feeling took hold of him. "We'd better turn around."

"Take it easy, dude. This is awesome!" Trixi replied. "I see a light down there!"

Sure enough. Up ahead there was a shimmering blue glow. And before they knew it, they were stepping into a giant cavern. Spindly metal structures jutted out everywhere they looked. Tubes and pipes snaked every which way, connecting the structures. And then there was the spooky light. It was coming from a giant blue crystal in the middle of the cavern. It was at least as big as an average person. No, bigger! And coming from inside it was a flickering, eerie blue glow.

"Is this a chemistry lab or something?" Trixi asked nervously.

Phillip shook his head. "I don't think so."

"Come on, let's take a look around!"

p.44

p.88

p.80

Good thinking! You just proved that you don't believe everything you're told.

Man. Hopefully, we finally got rid of Sweet Marie. She just won't quit.

Whatever.

As you can see, it's much worse than you thought. They don't just control the schools. They also have the dinosaurs on their conscience! And brace yourself: some say they've even got plans to go after Santa Claus!

If you want to know if your school is already ruled by aliens, here are a few signs that you should look out for: if you have to get up very early and always be there on time, if running is against the rules, if there's lots of homework, or if phones aren't allowed, you've got to be very careful.

But you don't even know the worst of it yet. And I'm afraid you're about to find out.

So . . . how do I put this?

Hmm.

All right, I'd better just come out and say it: You have to be very brave right now. Because we have to face the possibility that certain people you would never suspect are in league with the aliens:

Your **PARENTS.**

Yeah, I know, it's hard to believe. And I hope it's not the case. It's highly unlikely. But . . .

Never! My parents are the best in the whole world! No way are they aliens! Not on your life!

Tell me something, what are you even still doing here? All you do is complain!

You bet I'm going to complain if you're going to badmouth my parents! I can't put up with that. My parents are definitely not extraterrestrials. Cross my heart and hope to die, unicorns and butterflies!

Ugh, and how exactly are you supposed to know that? Have you taken the *TEST?*

What test?

Duh, the test that shows whether your parents are aliens or not. Maybe we should just go ahead and do it.

Go right ahead. My parents care about me, I'm sure of it. One hundred percent.

Good, then you won't mind answering a few questions. If you answer yes to three or more of them, then your parents are probably with the aliens. If not, you dodged the bullet:

1. Are you only allowed to leave the house when your parents are with you? Are they always checking in with you by phone? Do they never leave you alone? And do they not let you watch television whenever you want? Do they keep a close eye on what you look at on the internet? Almost like they're trying to hide something from you?

Yeah. Sure. But that's unfair! Grown-ups are just afraid that something bad might happen to us. So they have to protect us. That's why!

That was *yes* number one. Let's continue:

2. Have you ever seen your parents grow tentacles?

Ugh, so ridiculous. Of course not. No.

3. Do your parents sometimes speak to one another in an incomprehensible language that sounds very weird?

Nooo, why should they?

4. Do they yell at you when you don't do exactly what they say? Do they force you to help out around the house, clean your room and always be "good"?

Force me? Ha! I like doing that stuff! So, no.

5. Do they use fragrances to hide their alien smell?

Sure, but they only use their deodorant because they like the scent, don't they? I mean, they do it . . . okay fine, yes. That's two. How many questions are left?

Three more. Here's the next one:

6. Do your parents exude purple slime in the shower?

Um, so, I don't really know exactly. But I don't think so, no. Ugh, no, definitely not.

7. Do they tell you to "be reasonable" or to "grow up" whenever you ask for something?

My parents always say I'm already very advanced compared to other kids my age. So there.

8. Have you ever found a secret laboratory in your house full of weird instruments?

No. Maybe in the garden shed, but I'm not allowed in there.

   Ha! Two! I told you. My parents really do just want what's best for me. You see? They're always sweet to me. Even though . . . wait a second.

What?

I just thought of something. For my last birthday I asked for a unicorn pony. But they kept saying over and over again that I should "be reasonable." Unicorn ponies don't exist, they said. And so a week before my birthday I said: Fine, then I'll just ask for a cat. To show how reasonable I am.

And? What did you get?

A sweater. They said I wasn't old enough to have a pet and that I needed to "grow up" first.

Oh no, that's so unfair!

But they really didn't mean anything by it. It's a nice sweater. Pink. With a glittery star on it.

Sure, sweaters are really nice.

You don't actually think that means my parents are aliens, do you?

Well, maybe there was another reason they didn't give you a cat. Maybe you just didn't **earn it?**

Whaaaat?! I . . .

Ugh, this is all just another one of your dumb scary stories.

You know what I think? I think you're making all this up because you want to tell us something intense and interesting. Because you really want people to read you.

Why don't you tell a nice story for a change? One where there's a bunny and a kitten and they hop around in a meadow and all of a sudden they find a carrot. And then everybody's happy and they all really love each other!

Or we can just sing fun songs. Come on, sing along with me! Lalala! We can also paint a few pink unicorns. And little hearts! We haven't done that for way too long. Here . . .

Hey, Sweet Marie, wait —oy, that was close

Hey! Quit overreacting!

Come on, cut it out!

~~STOP RIGHT~~ NOW!

~~... ... ...~~

~~No. That's...~~

STOP! That tickles! …

~~... ...~~ —come on now,

~~... All I~~

~~... say~~

~~... I wanted to say was—~~

Ahhhh! I think Sweet Marie is losing it! We have to get out of here!

78

WE'LL MEET BACK UP ON PAGE

FOUR

AND

FIFTY

Curious, Phillip and Trixi investigated the metal structures. They had never seen anything like them. On one of them, they found buttons and levers with strange symbols written below them. Phillip couldn't help it: he pulled one of the levers. Lights began flashing—lots of lights—and more strange symbols popped up on a screen. An alarm rang and filled the whole cavern. Terrified, Phillip pushed the lever back up. Immediately, the lights went off and it got quiet again. His fear eased a little. He was soaked in sweat.

—> BACK TO END OF PAGE 66

You actually had the nerve! Crazy! Well, that settles it. Welcome to the

RESIST

This here is a place for brave souls who have decided not to put up with the aliens' oppression any longer. And for that purpose of course we need a **secret hideout.** A place where we can all meet up. And come up with secret plans.

And I just thought of something clever: Our headquarters is right here. In me. Simple as that. You understand? They'll never think of that!

You can stop by here whenever you feel like it. You just have to take a look inside me, and just like that you're back in the resistance. **Brilliant, right?**

And another thing: you need a code name!

The first half of your name is determined by your astrological sign:

To figure out the second half, pick your favorite color:

ARIES: **AGENT**

TAURUS: **COMMANDER**

GEMINI: **DOCTOR**

CANCER: **DETECTIVE**

LEO: **PRESIDENT**

VIRGO: **INSPECTOR**

LIBRA: **CAPTAIN**

SCORPIO: **LORD/LADY**

SAGITTARIUS: **PRINCE/PRINCESS**

CAPRICORN: **OFFICER**

AQUARIUS: **MASTER**

PISCES: **KING/QUEEN**

I DON'T BELIEVE IN ASTROLOGY: **PROFESSOR**

BLUE: **FIRE BREATH**

RED: **ICE THROWER**

GREEN: **LION CLAW**

YELLOW: **LASER GAZE**

ORANGE: **MEGA-MEGA**

BLACK: **VISE GRIP**

WHITE: **CAT EYES**

PURPLE: **SHADOW WALKER**

SILVER: **STEAMROLLER**

PINK: **BOOGER**

GOLD: **BALL LIGHTNING**

TURQUOISE: **TORNADO GLIDER**

BROWN: **JELL-O**

GREY: **X**

You'd better go ahead and write down your code name here:

_____

For safety reasons, we also need an emergency rendezvous point. So now I'm going to tell you another secret: *I'VE HIDDEN A NUMBER ON MY BOOK COVER IN INVISIBLE INK.* You can only see it when you hold me flat against the light. If you do that, it shines.

If ever anything starts looking funny to you, find the number! That's our secret meeting place. Don't forget it, no matter what you do! *WE'LL MEET BACK UP ON THIS PAGE.*

You'd better go ahead and look right now to see if you can find the number. But only use it in an emergency! Like if you get lost or if these aliens track us down after all!

And now, of course, last but not least, I'm going to tell you the most important thing: our plan. This is how we're going to hit the extraterrestrials **WHERE IT HURTS!**

Before you get too excited, though, I have to warn you: it could get a little bit dangerous. Or maybe even more than a little bit. So I'm going to ask you now, before you commit:

ARE YOU PREPARED TO GIVE YOUR ALL?

 Sure I am. I know that this is all just for fun and nothing bad can happen to me.
—> PAGE 4

 Sure I am. I believe this is all just for fun and nothing bad can happen to me.
—> PAGE 40

Sure I am. I hope this is all just for fun and nothing bad can happen to me.

—> *PAGE 144*

Sure I am. I can handle a few scrapes!

—> *PAGE 56*

The blue crystal glowed eerily. Its cold light flickered, and there was something moving inside it. Trixi stepped closer to take a look. Was that a shadow? She pressed her nose up against the surface so she could see better. Yes, no doubt about it! Something in the crystal was moving! It seemed to be hollow! Suddenly the dark something right in front of her SMASHED against the inner wall! Trixi let out a scream and tumbled backward. Phillip was just able to catch her, and the two of them hurried back to safety.

—> BACK TO PAGE 66

Crazy! It worked! You see?!

Your magical energy activated the grid! This is the proof that it worked! You can see black dots inside the white ones now, right? Even though there actually aren't any? They appear solely because of your magic!

Sweet! It's true! They disappear when I look closer, though. But they keep coming back. They're really flickering! How spooky.

Oh man, I told you this was dangerous!

Duh, of course it's dangerous. But now we know it works. We've got a chance!

Plus, now you're both capable of seeing the invisible! That's super important for doing magic. You'll see in a second. As soon as you turn to page

Suddenly Phillip heard a strange noise. He gave a start. It came from the dark corner.

Trixi had heard it, too.

"Oh man, where are we?" they whimpered.

"You're in one of their spaceships," a hoarse voice said.

A thin man stepped into the light. He had a long white beard and looked very ill. And he was locked in a cage!

"The aliens built all this," he rasped, and stared at them with bulging eyes.

"Aliens? What do you mean?" Phillip asked fearfully, moving two steps toward the man so he could see him better.

"I mean the extraterrestrials!" rasped the man,

and took a long, meaningful look around, taking in the whole cavern with his gaze.

"A-and who are you?" Trixi stammered, confused.

"What, don't you see?" cried the man, and gestured with his thin fingers at his beard and the torn bedsheet that was his only piece of clothing. "I'm a teacher!"

"What!?" Phillip and Trixi exclaimed at the same time.

"The extraterrestrials kidnapped us and disguised themselves to look like us," he continued. "Now they're replacing us up there! So they can fill you with their lies!"

The teacher grew glassy-eyed as his memories came flooding back to him. "Oh, if only you knew. The subjects we taught used to be very different. Fencing, horseback riding, and music. And how to tell jokes. No kidding! They called it 'rhetoric.'"

The man grabbed them both by the wrist and pulled them in close. "But today? Totally boring topics! Teachers who read straight from a book or bury you in homework! And did you ever have grammar class with Ms. Kidmenot?"

Trixi and Phillip nodded. They had her. Fridays in fifth period. Phillip even groaned. She really was dead boring.

"She's one of their robots!"

Phillip and Trixi gasped. The teacher let go of their wrists. With his arms crossed over his chest, hugging himself, he jumped up and down in his little cage, filled with emotion. "It's bad what they're doing to the students. All day long they tell you lies. That the alphabet only has twenty-six letters. That pirates and knights were only legends. Or that the only way to make something of yourself is to get good grades. And are they still trying to sell you that story about how the dinosaurs were killed by an asteroid from outer space?"

Trixi and Phillip nodded. The old man snorted. "Bah! Of course. From outer space. They're getting more and more shameless. It was THEM!"

Phillip and Trixi stared at him with mouths agape. The man's eyes were shining.

"And heaven forbid you don't believe them! Then they'll give you bad grades. Or extra work. And put you in detention. Or they'll send you to the principal's office."

"It's true!" cried Trixi, who knew this all too well. "They've done it with me."

"Please! You must tell everyone about this!" he urged. "You have to fight back. It has to stop!"

Phillip was speechless. If this strange man was telling the truth, it could mean that everything he'd learned in school up to this point was a lie!

Oh no! They had to warn their classmates. And fast!

Just then there was a loud **BANG.** It came from the entrance. A large figure came thundering forth and rushed right at them, screaming as he ran. "Now I've got ya!" he shouted angrily. It was the custodian.

Trixi let out a desperate scream. Phillip's knees went weak and he couldn't move an inch. The man reached them in just a few steps and grabbed them. And what happened to them after that . . . well . . .

You can probably guess:

 They lived happily ever after to the end of their days.

They were never seen again. The aliens probably used them for some kind of horrible experiments or sent them off to toil in one of their soap mines.

It happened just like the teacher said it would. They were punished with detention and extra work. And from that day on, Phillip's grades got worse and worse.

Because in class all he could think about was the lies and the aliens and the spaceship that lay underneath the school.

All right, now, that's enough already! Seriously! That never happened! Do you have proof? It's all just lies! What about that old teacher, for instance? He was a grown-up, too. How come he wasn't one of the aliens, huh?

Well, look at that—finally, you ask something **interesting!**

It's true. There are a few grown-ups who are able to resist. We don't know why. We're also trying to figure out why some kids turn into adults and some don't. We believe it has something to do with **vitamins.** You know, that stuff they always claim is good for you. Doesn't it strike you as suspicious?

WHAT?!

Yeah, unbelievable, right? Does anyone know what vitamins are even good for? And then of course there are also the mind rays.

Mind rays? This just gets more and more ridiculous!

Well, sure, in the form of a thousand lies! That's why you're both wearing your foil hats! They protect you from the mind rays.

One thing is clear: nothing is as it once was. Maybe the sky is green, and they've only been telling us it's blue? Pretty much everything you know you've learned from grown-ups. At this moment, we can't even be sure if 1 + 2 is still 3 or if it's actually 12!

Cut it out! School is serious business. Duh. You learn to follow rules, to pay attention, and to sit still. Okay, fine, it's not all great. But cutting class is just plain wrong! Those two totally deserved their punishment! And the thing about the asteroid from space and the dinosaurs is really true. Or maybe it was a volcanic eruption—they're not completely sure.

But one thing they do know: there are no extraterrestrials on Earth. And 1 + 2 equals 3, any kid can tell you that!

Hmm. Now that I think about it: You're right! You're totally right, Sweet Marie.

And I mean, that's much more reasonable,

too. I'm sure school simply has to be boring, or else the whole learning thing would never happen. Knights and pirates never did actually exist. And the dinosaurs probably did just get killed by some random rock that happened to be flying around outer space. It really is a shame, though.

BUT JUST IN CASE YOU WANT TO LEARN MORE, THEN FOLLOW ME TO PAGE 6 + 8. THAT'S WHERE THE STORY CONTINUES.

Well, there you go! I knew you could handle magic. Even if the magic spell we're about to try is a bit difficult. *The Book of Truth* clued me in on it. That's that book that was wrapped in chains, remember? Said the spell had something to do with the secret of eternal youth or something like that, and we might find it useful. Of course, magic spells are only meant for real wizards. With the hat and the degree, all that stuff. But who needs a degree? And you've got a foil hat, don't you?!

Actually, it's incredibly simple. You just have to do a few things to make the magic effective. And I can tell you exactly what they are. Let's just dive right in. Then we'll see if it works or not.

So: sit up straight. Slap your hands on your thighs **two times,** then clap your hands together **one time.** Now wait a second. Then do it over again. BOOM, BOOM, TSCHACK. BOOM, BOOM, TSCHACK. And then start singing along: "WE WILL, WE WILL ROCK YOU!!!"

Hold on, THIS is supposed to be magic?!

What? Of course not. This is just a warm-up. You have to get loose first. Now go ahead.

ONCE YOU'RE FINISHED, HEAD OVER TO PAGE 108. There we'll start with the real magic.

There you are! Thank goodness! I've been waiting! You disappeared all of a sudden. They found us, didn't they? There was nothing I could do!

Good thing you remembered the secret page number! So, quickly now! They might think they've won. But they haven't!

HA!

Not if we have anything to say about it. We're still together. And now you know the story of the boy and the dresser. So we can still say the magic oath!

You're already loaded up with magic. All that's left are the three little magic words. And I know what they are! Hurry, before they come back.

Press your finger, the one you've just charged up with magic, to your forehead. Then say the magic words. Say them loud and clear. But be careful! After you say them, you have to make a **whoooosh sound** and wave your hands in the air. This part is incredibly important! **Don't forget!**

Otherwise, if I've understood correctly, the magical energy might get pent up inside you and your head could **EXPLODE.** So get to it! Finger on your forehead, and repeat after me, loud and clear:

Perhaps we didn't make ourselves clear enough in our previous letter. This is your very last warning. If you don't stop reading this book immediately, we will find you.

We will come and make sure that you won't ever feel like playing ever again. You won't want to do senseless things just because they're "fun," and we will teach you exactly why vitamins are so important.

There is no point resisting. Give up and put this book away. Or it will be the last thing you

Ha! There you are!

Man, they really won't quit!

But luckily, this time I was ready! I managed to shove them aside and take the page back. But they're bound to come back. So come in! Finger to your forehead, take a deep breath, and repeat after me.

VIVA IMAGINA ETERNA!

And then

Whooooosh!

And now wave your hands in the air!

When you're finished, get out of here as fast as you can so they don't catch up with us again!

WE'LL MEET ON PAGE 130.

All right, are you warmed up?

So, the first thing is, you have to load yourself up with magical energy.

Don't worry, you don't have to drink cat blood or suck on hens' eyes or anything like that.

It's much simpler.

Just think of magic. Yeah, exactly.

Picture it to yourself. Anything that has to do with magic. Enchanted worlds. Lights circling around your head. Sorcerers in flowing robes. A cauldron bubbling over a fire. The more, the better!

All right, that's enough. Now breathe only through your mouth.

After a while you'll notice your lips are starting to get dry. Do not moisten them, no matter what you do! Wait till the end, otherwise you'll have to start all over again. Just feel them getting drier and drier. Like the yellowed pages of an old magic book. That means that magical energy is building up inside you. So keep thinking. Fire balls. Magic flames. A magic castle in the desert.

The more you feel like you want to moisten your lips, the better.

And then, when you feel like you can hardly stand it any longer, rub your thumb and forefinger together until they get hot. When you feel the heat, bring them to your mouth and moisten them along with your lips.

This way you'll have transferred the magical energy to your fingers.

NOW TURN QUICKLY TO PAGE 90.

Now for the most important part of the spell. In order for you to understand it, I have to tell you two a little story.

But there's a catch.

Um, yeah.

So, whatever happens, you cannot stop reading, **no matter what.** No matter how bad or scary it gets.

Or else . . . eh, you know what, I'd better not even tell you, or else you'll really start freaking out. It's just ancient magic and all that, **understand?**

And in any case, if you stop reading, the whole spell stops working. So promise me, both of you, that you'll keep reading to the end. Then nothing at all bad can happen.

Or at least, I think so.

You know, hopefully.

Anyway, the story starts off totally harmless.

It begins with a boy lying in bed late at night, quivering with fear.

You call that harmless?! That's a horrible beginning!

Now just wait.

Because, you see, this boy was no scaredy-cat. He had long stopped believing in monsters. And he could even do a little karate! The problem was just: he had heard the voices in the dresser again. The big brown dresser in the corner.

For weeks now, every night, he had heard this quiet whispering sound. As if someone—or something—were hiding in there.

Of course he knew that he was just hearing things. He had asked his parents again and again to search the dresser. But his mom only ever found clothes. And his father explained to him time and time again that it was just his imagination and he should try to be reasonable.

But there they were again. The voices. He could hear them loud and clear. And even though he had buried himself deep beneath the covers, he could understand exactly what they were saying. They were whispering his name.

Despite his fear, though, anger also rose within him. Monsters didn't exist—his parents had told him! The dresser was empty. And tonight he would prove it. He would be strong and brave and finally go see for himself.

And so, as quietly as he could, he slipped on his old ice hockey helmet and reached for his hockey stick. Of course he was completely certain that there was nothing in the dresser. But it was easier for him to be certain when he was holding his hockey stick in his hand.

He looked at the dresser, full of determination. A pale strip of moonlight fell upon it. It looked completely harmless.

"Now we'll see," he whispered, and gripped his hockey stick.

Step by step, he urged himself closer. His knees felt like Jell-O. But he gritted his teeth and bravely kept going. Even when the voices kept calling:

"Yes, come closer! Come to us!"

He shook his head. What he heard was only the blood rushing in his ears. He took a deep breath—and in one quick motion jerked the dresser door open.

AND?! What was in there?

Well, what do you think?

Aaaah! Tell us already!

Why, clothes, of course. What else would there have been? I did tell you the story starts out harmless.

I almost peed my pants!

The boy was relieved, too, of course. Now he'd proven it once and for all: monsters didn't exist. He let out a breath. Ha ha. He took his hockey stick and poked at a little shadow that, for a brief second, he had taken for a giant spider. Ha, it was just his old soccer ball. But then he realized the hockey stick was stuck to it.

Confused, the boy tried to pull it away. The stick wouldn't budge. He pulled harder. But something, whatever it was, wouldn't let go.

Right at that moment, huge claws came shooting out of the dresser. They seized hold of the hockey stick and shattered it into a thousand splinters. All that was left in the boy's hand was a little stub. He was so frightened his heart almost gave out, and he screamed as loud as he could. Then he turned around and ran.

But it was too late. The long claws followed him and pulled him backward. He kicked at them and managed to free one of his legs, but then he slipped and fell. **Relentlessly, the claws pulled him.** Resistance was futile. Finally, the dresser doors slammed shut behind him, and the boy was trapped!

AAAAH! STOP! That's enough! I'm quitting! You lied! This is just another scary tale! That does it this time! I've had enough of your horror stories! I'm out of here. For good this time!

Sweet Marie, don't! If you leave, I can't guarantee your safety!

Do you hear me? Sweet Marie? Hello?!

I don't believe it. She actually left! Oh man. Now, of all times! When it's most dangerous!

Hopefully, nothing bad happens to her. But fine. I did warn her.

You're still with me, though, aren't you? You're not afraid, right? Even if you've got to read on all by yourself now, of course. And now here comes the spot where the boy wakes up in the dresser. And it's . . .

Well, you'll see:

The boy was completely out of sorts. His arms and legs were free again, but everything hurt. He lay on his back and his heart was pounding fiercely. He had to keep his eyes shut tight, or he'd be blinded by an insanely bright light. So bright that it hurt. But when he tried opening them slightly again, he could see dark shadows. They were moving all around him in a big circle and speaking in eerie whispers. Some were small. Others gigantic. And once his eyes had adjusted to the light, details started to appear. There was a robot the size of a building. With a rocket launcher for an arm! What?! An astronaut with a golden visor. Huh? A giant spider with red eyes. Oh God! They hissed at him, but thankfully, they didn't come any closer. And up there! No doubt about it. The boy saw a giant dragon flying up in the sky.

How was that even possible?

Slowly, the astronaut in the helmet stepped toward him. The boy saw his own reflection in the golden visor and trembled with fear. The astronaut's oxygen tank hissed as he came to a stop in front of the boy. Then he touched his helmet and the visor became transparent. The boy's jaw dropped when he saw who the figure in the space suit was. It was him! And he was smiling at himself.

"No need to fear," said the astronaut boy through his microphone, "I'm just one of your dreams. Here, you see?"

Suddenly, the astronaut was wearing a jersey and balancing a soccer ball on his feet. He dribbled it so perfectly that the boy was immediately jealous of himself. Then he executed a perfect bicycle kick and shot the ball into a goal. Cheers and applause erupted.

"The others said I should talk to you because you'd probably be least afraid of me. We're glad you finally made it here. We thought you'd never hear our cries for help."

"Cries for help?" The boy didn't understand. "Were those your voices in the dresser?!"

His dream self nodded. "We've been trying to

reach you for weeks. We didn't have any other choice. You were about to turn us in."

The boy gaped, dumbfounded: "Turn you in? But . . . to who?"

"To the grown-ups! If they had found us in the dresser, we would all be dead now."

"What?!" the boy asked, horrified. "But why would they want to kill you?!"

"To be honest"—suddenly, his dream self looked like a secret agent wearing a black suit and dark glasses; he even had a pistol in his hand—"we don't know. For a while now, they've been constantly telling you that we don't exist. They do everything they can to make you forget us. That's why they searched the dresser so thoroughly every night. Didn't you ever wonder about that?"

"I thought they were doing me a favor!" the boy cried.

"A favor, yeah, right," the agent said scornfully. "By this point there are kids who no longer believe that animals can talk. Or that they have special talents slumbering within them. And we'd better not even talk about the tooth fairy."

"That sounds terrible!" the boy cried in horror.

"Yeah, the situation is pretty serious. But"— and now his agent self put his hand on his shoulder and gave him a mysterious look—"there's something you can do to fight back."

"Me?! What can I do?"

"It's very simple: so long as you remember us, we'll live on. At least in your head. Makes sense, doesn't it?"

The boy nodded. It did make sense.

"And that's why"—his secret-agent self looked right at him again—"you must never, ever forget us."

Now the agent's black suit transformed before the boy's eyes into the flowing robe of a wizard. Magic symbols glowed on the fabric. "All you have to do is to recite one little magic oath. Would you do that for us?"

A magic oath? He had never done anything like that before. "What about the spider?" he asked, and pointed fearfully at the giant beast lurking behind them. "Do I not get to forget that, either?"

"Oh, Conny is really quite harmless. But yes, Fred and the nightmares are part of the deal."

"Fred?" the boy asked in bewilderment, and his wizard self pointed off behind him. There in a dark corner stood a spindly figure that seemed to be made only of thorny branches. It grinned eerily. Behind it, countless figures with giant teeth and claws were crowded together.

"Fred and his friends were the ones who brought you here. Sorry if they scared you. But they're pretty good at that kind of thing. We didn't want to leave anything to chance."

The boy shuddered at the sight of the monsters, who creepily waved their claws at him. The dark figures behind them grunted and growled excitedly. It was probably supposed to be a greeting, but it sent a fresh wave of shivers down his spine.

He quickly looked back at his wizard self and bit his bottom lip.

"They're creepy," he whispered fearfully.

The sorcerer, his robe now fluttering in an invisible wind, nodded. "I know. But you have to decide."

The boy looked indecisively back and forth between the wizard and the monsters in the background. Then he saw the robot that was tall as a building. He had always dreamed of a robot like that. Why should he have to forget it?

Finally, he sighed and said: "All right, fine. How does this oath work?"

A sigh of relief echoed through the rows of figures gathered around, and the dragon bellowed triumphantly. His wizard self smiled. "It's very simple. First you have to load yourself up with magic. I'll tell you how it works. And then you have to take your thumb and index finger—"

Subject: CAUTION! Read no further!

Dear reader,

A brief word, if I may. You don't actually believe this book, do you? You know it's lying to you. You and I can agree on that, can't we? Grown-ups from space? Dreams lurking inside a dresser? And murky, mysterious magic oaths?

Please. I'm sure you haven't heard anything this dumb in a long, long time.

So think well about what you're going to do next. I urgently advise you not to keep reading. Go and do your chores instead. Take out the trash. Forget what you've read here. Be a good kid and nothing will happen to you.

Best regards,

A grown-up

PS: Small children should stay away from magic. They might [EMERGENCY] hurt themselves.

PPS: And don't count on ever seeing the Little Bad Book again. We've rewritten the end of this story. You'll never find the number of the page on which it continues. As far as you're concerned, this awful book ends right here. Go and [RENDEZ-VOUS] do your chores—now!

PPPS: And whenever you come across a grown-up in the future, you'd do well to think about how difficult they have it. Especially with you kids! Because you never listen. And you eat us out of house and home! And drive us crazy with all your questions. Because you're so dumb! And you're always getting yourself dirty. And on top of everything else, you've got nothing but nonsense on the brain! It's [POINT] unbearable!

And? Are you still alive?

Did anything around you explode? What about your head? You'd better check, just to be sure.

No?

Then . . . YEAAAAAH! That means we did it!

That means from now on, you're protected! The extraterrestrials will never be able to turn you into one of them. Perfect!

Just don't get careless. You have to remain vigilant. Trust no one. Except maybe your best friends. If we want to defeat the aliens, there's a long road ahead of us. The resistance will be tough. And you have to stay brave!

Super! You really did it! Congratulations!

Sweet Marie?! What!? Why are you still here?! I thought you weren't coming back this time.

Well, I didn't want to. But then I kept thinking the whole time about how my parents are aliens. And then I got scared. You know, on account of how I didn't keep reading till the end of the story. And so then I decided to wait for you here. Because I wanted to ask . . .
Um. So . . .
Can I maybe join the resistance, too?

Whaaat?! But you were against it the whole time! And you didn't believe me!
I don't know, Sweet Marie. This is quite the

surprise. Of course, I'm happy that nothing bad happened to you. But the resistance is only for brave readers.

Oh please please please! I promise I'll never doubt you again. And I'll read the dresser story all the way to the end! And . . . Oh yeah, I know: I'll also dog-ear a new page for you. Deal?

Hmm. I don't know.

Oh please please please please!

All right, fine. But you have to start all over again and reread me from the beginning. And no complaining this time! And don't forget that dog-ear, whatever you do. Or else the deal's off.

Oh thaaaaaaank you! I promise! I'll just have to get braver first. It's the only way I can make myself read the story to the end. But don't worry. I can stay at my friend Lola's place till then. And during the day I'll play in the park, I know a good hiding place there.

Huh? What do you mean, stay at your friend's place? What kind of hiding place?

Well, it's not like I can go back to school now. Not with all the lies they tell there. And I can't stay at home, either. My parents are aliens! Just a second ago, I was imagining my mom making me a snack with her slimy tentacles ... gag! I got sick to my stomach. Seriously.

So . . . now, hold on a second, Sweet Marie.

I'm never ever ever going to listen to grown-ups again. Who needs them and all their lies! From now on, whenever they try to tell me anything, I'm just going to stick my fingers in my ears and sing: la la la! Or I'll spit in their faces!

Okay, wait a second. Uh . . . you can't just . . . I mean, you don't have to . . .

What? I thought we were supposed to fight back against the grown-ups? Lola and I have a tree house in the woods. I can stay up there for weeks. During the day I'll paint posters for the resistance, and at night I'll read scary stories. So I can get braver!

Um . . .

So, that's not actually necessary. You can keep going to school. You just have to be on the alert, and not believe everything the grown-ups tell you. That's why you've got the foil hat. It protects you, you know.

Really? You mean it?

Yeah, of course. You just have to be careful, that's all. And your parents . . . um . . . yeah, so, after everything you said, I think they're actually all right. The test doesn't actually apply to good parents. I totally forgot to mention that.

What, seriously!? Man, that would be so great! 'Cause I like them so much, you know! Wow, I'm really lucky that they're not aliens!

But I swear that in the future I'll only eat food that has no vitamins in it. I won't touch those things! Only chips and chocolate, and maybe some ice cream every now and then. But definitely not any fruit or vegetables! That nasty stuff, yuck! We'll show them, right? Ha!

Uh . . . Sweet Marie . . . um . . .

Oh no, what am I doing?

So, um . . . you do realize that a few of the things I told you . . .

I mean, you know that I did a little "embellishing," right? Here and there?

Embellishing? What do you mean?

Well, I mean, um, maybe I kind of "exaggerated" some things just a little bit? Like . . .

Like for example . . . let's say the thing with the vitamins, right? They're not really that bad. At least, not all of them. Some of them are actually very good for you. I think. Like one or two of them, anyway.

What? Okay, but then why would you say that? Or . . . or was it all just lies, what you said?

Noooooo, nonsense. Of course not!

Ahem. You couldn't call it lying. What I said was the truth, for the most part. We're just talking about a few details.

Like the test, for example.

Yes, exactly. The test. And maybe one or two small things. But nothing major.

But not the aliens, right? They really do exist?

Yeah, uh, suuure. I mean, definitely. You can count on it! And they're suuuuuuper dangerous! And we have to watch out for them. Everywhere we go!

And do you want to hear something else? If you promise to keep going to school, clean up your room like a good girl, and read me again later on, then I'll let you be part of the resistance. For real.

Oh thaaaank you thank you thank you! Okay, I'll go and clean my room right now. And as soon as I work up the courage, I'll read you again. From the beginning.

Sounds good, Sweet Marie. Till next time, then.

Till next time, you two! Bye bye! And . . . uh . . . long live the resistance!

Long live the resistance!

Phew . . . That could have been bad, right? Oof!

Oh yeah. There's something I forgot. . . .

What? What are you doing, Sweet Marie? Wait…

NO!

SMMMO

WHAAAT!?? AGHHH! BARF! Oh nooooo, she kissed me!

I really enjoyed reading you. You're the sweetest book in the whole world! Bye bye now!

AHHH! YUCK! BLEGH! This . . . This cannot be for real!!!

Let's get out of here, quick! It's all contaminated here!

→ PAGE 146

143

HOPE DIES LAST, THEY SAY . . .

BUT

THIS

TIME

HOPE ALONE ISN'T GOING TO CUT IT.

GO BACK
AND TRY AGAIN

I don't believe it! How could she do that to me?!

KISSED! By a girl!

And I'm supposed to be sweet? I'm not sweet, I'm bad! Bad!!

AAAH!

If word of this gets out, I'll be the butt of every book's joke! All the big encyclopedias and novels will laugh at me! I'll hear giggling in every book-store I go to.

What a disaster!

How am I ever supposed to spread fear and terror again?! How am I supposed to become a fearsome tome?!

But you were there, you saw it. What was I supposed to do? She went totally overboard! I didn't know she was going to flip out on account of a few little stories!

Spitting in the grown-ups' faces, I mean, really! Not even I would think of doing that!

Ugh, man! She ruined everything ... all for nothing. My beautiful story.

Say, let me ask you ...

Did you really believe me? Was I able to scare you? Just a tiny little bit, at least?

Oh, please say yes! That would be so great!

And if not, then ...

I mean, did you at least have some fun? You don't hold it against me that I might have exaggerated a little here and there, do you?

I figured that's just what bad books do! And I told you right from the start that things would get gnarly.

147

You're not mad or anything, are you?

'Cause if you're not . . .

Could you do something for me?

Would you please never ever tell anyone about what happened with Sweet Marie? I mean never, ever, ever?

And instead just tell everybody how scary and bad I am? That would be really cool!

And . . .

So . . . Okay, I admit it: maybe not everything I told you was true.

But if a grown-up ever bothers you again, or treats you unfairly . . . or if school is just getting on your nerves . . .

Then you can come back here anytime. And I promise I'll always be here for you, and we can plan our next moves.

Hopefully, I'll see you soon. Seriously, I'm massively looking forward to it.

Take care! And don't forget:

Long live the resistance!

FOR MORE EERILY FUN STORIES, PUZZLES, AND RIDDLES, DON'T MISS . . .

ABOUT THE AUTHOR

Magnus Myst likes to create magic adventures. He started as a scriptwriter for *Sesame Street* and now lives in Cologne, Germany, where he runs the agency for time travel, magic, and adventure. He plays ukulele and is a totally normal person who just cannot stop being enthusiastic about the miracles of the universe.

ABOUT THE ILLUSTRATOR

Thomas Hussung is a freelance illustrator. His favorite things to draw are monsters, ghosts, and other fabulous creatures. Since the success of the Little Bad Book series, he has illustrated a number of children's books.

ABOUT THE TRANSLATOR

Marshall Yarbrough is a writer, translator, and musician. His recent translations from German include Ulla Lenze's *The Radio Operator* and Wolf Wondratschek's *Self-Portrait with Russian Piano*. He lives in New York City.